This
PJ BOOK
belongs to

_____

_____

PjLibrary®

JEWISH BEDTIME STORIES and SONGS

To Madaline Roth Weinstein and her husband, Neil

Text and illustrations copyright © 1992 by Patricia Polacco
All rights reserved. Published by Doubleday Books for Young Readers, an imprint of Random House
Children's Books, a division of Penguin Random House LLC, New York.

Doubleday and the colophon are registered trademarks of Penguin Random House LLC.

Visit us on the Web! rhcbooks.com

Educators and librarians, for a variety of teaching tools, visit us at
RHTeachersLibrarians.com

Library of Congress Cataloging-in-Publication Data
Polacco, Patricia.
Mrs. Katz and Tush / Patricia Polacco
p. cm.
"A Doubleday Book for Young Readers"
Summary: A long-lasting friendship develops between Larnel, a young African American, and Mrs.
Katz, a lonely Jewish widow, when Larnel presents Mrs. Katz with a scrawny kitten without a tail.
ISBN: 978-0-375-97211-9
[1. Friendship—Fiction.   2. Jews—Fiction.   3. African Americans—Fiction.   4. Cats—Fiction.]
I. Title.
PZ7.P75186Mr   1992
[E]—dc20
91018710

MANUFACTURED IN CHINA
10 9 8 7 6 5 4

031828.3K5/B1185A7

Patricia Polacco

Mrs. Katz and Tush

Doubleday Books
for Young Readers

Larnel didn't know Mrs. Katz very well, but almost every other day his mother stopped in to see her after work.

"Since her husband died, she's so alone," his mother had told him.

Mrs. Katz held tight to his mother's hand the day they looked at an old photo album. "That's my husband, Myron," said Mrs. Katz. "He came from Poland like me, a long time ago. We had such a life, such a life!" Then her voice broke.

"We had no children, and I'll be all alone for Hannukah and Passover."

Then she cried.

The next day Larnel stopped in to see her himself.

"I've been thinking," he said. "A cat had some kittens in the basement of our building. We found someone to take them all except this one. She's the runt. Nobody wants her because she is so ugly. She doesn't even have a tail."

"Ugly, you say," Mrs. Katz said. "My Myron was ugly, too, when he was little, but he grew up to be such a person!"

Mrs. Katz looked at the little kitten.

"Scrawny little *bubeleh* . . . so small . . . no tail," she said as she examined the kitten closely.

"I don't know," she said doubtfully. Then she saw the look on Larnel's face.

"Larnel, I'll take her!" she announced. "But only if you'll come and help me with her. I've never had a cat before."

Larnel promised.

"A good Yiddish name I'll give her," said Mrs. Katz. "Let's see, she has no tail—all you see is her tush. That's it! We'll call her Tush."

Little Tush grew healthy and strong.
Mrs. Katz cooked for her,
brushed her,
knitted toys for her,
and even read to her.
"Such a person," she'd say as she watched Tush play.
Mrs. Katz was in love.

Larnel kept his promise. He visited Mrs. Katz and Tush every day after school. There was always a fresh-baked kugel and a tall glass of milk waiting for him. But as much as he grew to love Tush, he also loved to listen to Mrs. Katz talk about the old country and the way times used to be.

"I come from Warsaw. That's in Poland, you know. I came here to work sewing dresses in the garment district for my cousin Moyshe. I didn't speak one word of English!"

"Then how did you talk to people?" asked Larnel.

"I didn't," she answered. "A lot, I cried in those days . . . until I met Myron. He asked me to marry him after he tasted my kugel!"

"I believe that!" Larnel said as he ate some.

"Myron and I used to vacation in the Catskills—a borscht resort, you know, a place for Jews to stay."

"You mean Jews couldn't stay anywhere they wanted to?" Larnel asked.

Mrs. Katz didn't answer. Instead she went to a trunk and pulled out some old clothes.

"My grandma told me about places she couldn't stay, either," Larnel said softly.

"Larnel, your people and mine are alike, you know. Trouble, we've seen. Happiness, too. Great strength we've had. You and I are alike, so much alike!

"Now where was I? Oh yes, the Catskills! We used to dress every Sunday and have a costume ball," said Mrs. Katz.

Then she put a record on the record player. It was old and scratched.

"You hear that, Larnel?" she said. "That is what we used to dance to. It's a dance from my homeland. Here, I'll show you."

They whirled around the room and laughed and giggled.

As the weeks passed, Larnel spent more and more time with Mrs. Katz.

"Since you are almost family to me, Larnel," she said one day, "I want you should come with me to say kaddish for my Myron. I know you're not Jewish, but Myron would have liked you. You're such a person, Larnel!"

At the cemetery she read from her book.

Then she asked Larnel to put a small rock on top of Mr. Katz's headstone.

"We do this to remember," she said softly. "Shalom, my Myron," she murmured and wiped tears from her face.

On the way home she announced, "Kugel! Such a kugel I baked for you today, Larnel!"

"Hurry—Tush will be worried for us," she said as they walked.

When they got home, they called and called for Tush, but she didn't come.

They looked everywhere for her. Suddenly Mrs. Katz gasped. The window to the fire escape was open.

"Oh no!" she cried. "I forgot to shut the window before I left! Poor *bubeleh*! She has never been outside!"

"We'll find her." Larnel tried to reassure her.

"She has been acting strange lately," Mrs. Katz said through her tears. "She has been trying to get out, but I was afraid that she would get hit by a car!"

"I'll find her, Mrs. Katz," Larnel said. "I won't let you down!"

It was getting dark.

First Mrs. Katz and Larnel looked around their building.

Then they went everywhere on their street.

They left notes on doors, telephone poles, and fences.

They asked everyone who lived nearby, but no one had seen little Tush.

That night it stormed.

There was rain, awful, awful rain!

Mrs. Katz hardly slept as she thought about her little *kattileh*.

"She's such a person . . . such a person!" she whispered.

Larnel worried most of the night, too.

What will Mrs. Katz do! he thought.

"Please, God, bring that little cat back to her," he said softly into his pillow.

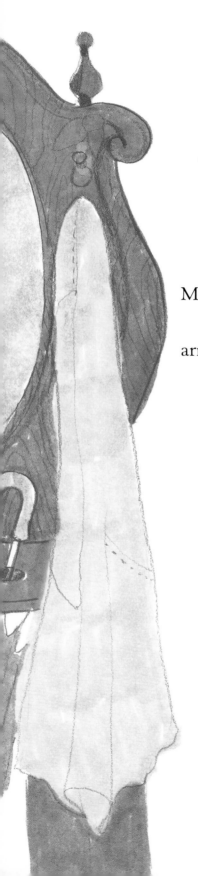

A loud knock on the front door awoke Mrs. Katz.

It was Larnel's father and two neighbors.

"Is this yours?" they asked.

"My *bubeleh*! Little *kattileh*!" Mrs. Katz exclaimed.

"We found her in the back alley, soaking wet and hungry," Mr. Moore said.

"Thank you, thank you!" Mrs. Katz said as she took Tush in her arms.

After a while, Tush no longer had the least desire to go outside again. But she slept a lot, even when Larnel came over to play with her.

"It was at my aunt Havelah's Passover seder that I met Myron. Did you know that?" Mrs. Katz asked as she looked at Larnel. "What good times they were, with lots and lots of family. Now it's just me," she said softly.

"Could I have Passover dinner with you?" asked Larnel.

"I thought you would never ask!" she exclaimed as she hugged him close. "Such a seder I'll prepare for you!"

"Passover is a time for good food," Mrs. Katz shouted as they edged their way through the crowd in the deli.

"Like your people, my people were slaves, too. They lived in a country where they didn't want to be. They wanted freedom so much that they prayed to God to help them. So he sent an angel—an angel that brought death and sadness to the houses of our captors. But the angel did not visit the houses of my people."

"How did the angel know where the Jews lived?" Larnel asked.

"They marked the doors. Then the angel passed over. Passed over, Larnel, that's why we call this time of celebration Passover!"

"So, Larnel, we have a big feast to celebrate, but we also remember those who had to suffer so we could be free," Mrs. Katz said. "Part of the dinner is sad and part of it is happy!"

As Larnel helped get out the linens and china, Mrs. Katz said, "You see this tablecloth, this was our wedding *chuppa*, our canopy. For all these years we have used it for holy days and celebrations."

"How come you have so many different dishes?" Larnel asked.

"Because some Jews don't eat dairy and meat off of the same dishes," she answered.

When they sat down to seder together, Mrs. Katz lit two candles and waved her hands over them. She read from her book, said prayers, then smiled and said, "Let the feast begin!"

They drank red wine and water. They ate bitter herbs, lamb, and chicken. They also had gefilte fish and spicy chopped apples with potato pancakes.

"This bread looks like a cracker!" Larnel exclaimed.

"We call it matzoh, dear. We eat it at Passover. It's flat because there is no yeast in it, so it doesn't rise."

"Larnel, I have hidden one piece of the matzoh. If you can find it, I have a surprise for you!"

The surprise was a hand-knit sweater that she had made just for him!

The next day Mrs. Katz yelled out her back window to Larnel.

"Come quick, already . . . something wonderful!"

Larnel and his parents rushed to her door.

"The angel of death passed over, but the angel of life didn't! Mazel tov, Tush! Four babies—at last I am a bubee!"

As the years passed, Mrs. Katz, Tush, and her descendants became part of Larnel's family.

There were graduations, weddings, new babies, and finally a kaddish.

Larnel stood in front of the headstone.

He read from her book.

He placed a small rock on top of her headstone.

Then he, his wife, and their children read the inscription together.

MRS. KATZ, OUR BUBEE . . . SUCH A PERSON.

creative
Wedding Showers

handmade invitations ♡ decorations ♡ games
planning tips ♡ menu ideas and more!

Laurie Dewberry

North Light Books
Cincinnati, Ohio
www.artistsnetwork.com

09 08 07 06 05   5 4 3 2 1

Library of Congress Cataloging-in-Publication Data
Dewberry, Laurie
    Creative wedding showers / by Laurie Dewberry.
      p. cm.
    Includes index.
    ISBN 1-55870-710-7
     1. Showers (Parties) 2. Weddings.   I. Title

GV1472.7.S5D48 2005
793.2--dc22

Editors
  Tonia Davenport
  Christine Doyle
  Jessica Gordon
Designer
  Leigh Ann Lentz
Layout Artists
  Kathy Gardner
  Leigh Ann Lentz
Production Coordinator
  Robin Richie
Stylist
  Janet A. Nickum
Stylist Assistant
  Nora Fink
Photographers
  Christine Polomsky
  Tim Grondin
  Al Parrish
Photography Assistant
  Kim Bock
Author photo on page 3
  Michelle Brown

METRIC CONVERSION CHART

TO CONVERT	TO	MULTIPLY BY
Inches	Centimeters	2.54
Centimeters	Inches	0.4
Feet	Centimeters	30.5
Centimeters	Feet	0.03
Yards	Meters	0.9
Meters	Yards	1.1
Sq. Inches	Sq. Centimeters	6.45
Sq. Centimeters	Sq. Inches	0.16
Sq. Feet	Sq. Meters	0.09
Sq. Meters	Sq. Feet	10.8
Sq. Yards	Sq. Meters	0.8
Sq. Meters	Sq. Yards	1.2
Pounds	Kilograms	0.45
Kilograms	Pounds	2.2
Ounces	Grams	28.4
Grams	Ounces	0.04